The
Sunday Stories

A Flash Fiction Anthology

by Spencer Spalding

Spencer Spalding
The Sunday Stories
© 2020, Spencer Spalding
SFwordsmith.com Print Division
All rights reserved.

ISBN: 978-1-7367470-1-8

I would like to dedicate this work, and truly every word I write, to my late grandfather, a great man named Jack Francis Fisher III. He raised me to be a man of integrity and he always supported my passion for words. His ashes lay off the coast of California, near the Golden Gate Bridge, but his soul lives on through the values he instilled in me.

This one's for you, my friend.
I told you it would happen.

*"The Universe, which oftentimes
is thought of as a collection of things,
should truly be looked at as one entity that is
constantly ebbing and flowing in reaction to itself.
When one thing happens in your life,
this sends waves outward, and subsequently,
will return reactionary energy to you in kind."*

–Spencer Spalding

Contents

Preface

The Sunday Stories anthology was bred out of the midst of a global pandemic. Written on Sundays during the initial corona-virus-induced lockdown in San Francisco, California, this 18-week flash fiction series details various stories reflecting upon the human condition. All of these stories reside within an alternate universe which finds the Earth unknowingly approaching its surrender into a rapidly expanding Sun, nicknamed The Red Giant. With fiction set both before and after this calamitous event, The Sunday Stories weave an interlaced narrative driven by hope and the idea that humanity is something to be appreciated if nothing else.

Not everyone knows when the Earth may end.
It is what you make of your time here that truly matters.

Please enjoy,
The Sunday Stories

Echoes of the Night

Footsteps echoed down a darkened alleyway with splashes of lingering water leaving the sanctity of the once still puddle's confining depression. A second pair of echoes followed shortly thereafter, quicker than the first, gaining ground with each planted sole and its subsequent rock toward springing metatarsals.

Tanner's breathing became shorter as his anxiety increased, turning around the nearest corner, making a mad dash into the unknown but away from the fate which he knew would accompany his already diminishing pace and his horrible lung capacity. The Turkish gold cigarettes which he had once shared on those memorable do-nothing evenings with Sara now belabored his frantic gasps for air, draining the strength from his muscles and sending shivers of pain through his tired tendons.

His pursuer however had seemingly boundless reserves of energy as he could hear the echoes closing in on him, the walls of the alleyway's encapsulating buildings towering over him and creating the perfect surface to reverberate the sounds of his impending doom. As the brick walls began to feel overwhelming, all he could imagine was the famous trash compactor scene from a galaxy far far away and Sara's unprompted laughter during it. The memory gave him a new hope and renewed vigor in his stride. His arms worked in tandem with each push-off and propelled him forward at his ultimate pace. A slight gap in the echoes of his enemy's pavement-pounding sneakers proved his sprinting's worth as he pulled away slightly.

The victory was not long-lasting. His lungs burned as the memories of those long October nights with a stogie trapped between his fingers flooded back into his mind, bringing glimpses of her as she would finish stories which were meaningless except for the fact that she was telling them to him before gesturing for him to pass her the brightly glowing nicotine candle which she had so kindly let him borrow. He could picture even now his breath in front of him on those chilly autumn nights filled with them basking in the moonlight.

Tanner looked up as he ran, noticing the presence of that same moon watching over him, and the clouds nearby which soon would cover its light, if but only for a moment or two. This was his chance. He pushed forward, pulling away just a little bit more before ducking around a corner as the clouds became his allies, enshrouding him in the darkness of the night. He ducked behind a nearby dumpster and hid, unable to see, but able to hear as his foe passed by him and the echoes faded into memories.

He stood once more, fumbling for the lighter she had let him borrow, and the pack of golds he was holding for her, putting one of the unlit cigarettes into his mouth and setting it ablaze… and just as he did, the echoes returned, but it was too late for a reaction as they were already upon him. Her face lit up in the now uncovered moonlight, and he could see her perfectly as she placed a tender kiss upon his cheek and said,

"Tag, you're it."

The Red Giant

I thought about the end of the world today.

The skies were blue and the wind, it blew, and the grass was green and through it came the breeze, and the bright white clouds traipsed across the horizon without a care in the world.

Whether or not there was man was not a necessary detail, for this is not the story of humankind, but of Mother Gaia, and she had existed before without men, and as such the end of her story cared little of their often beleaguered existence.

However, there was certainly the Sun, as it was clearly visible, growing ever more massive as Earth was drawn toward its welcoming embrace at the epicenter of a rapidly shrinking solar system.

The Sun had started undergoing an evolution into its next form, that of a massive red giant, as the humans had once named it, though whatever projections which were once seen on their mission control monitors paled in comparison to the reality of the next stage of life for their celestial body.

Mercury had gone quickly as the Sun expanded its territory, inconsequential was its surrender into the plasma of its star.

Venus had a week until it was tugged entirely away from its gravitational rotation around the Sun, but then it, like the Earth was now, moved toward the center, and eventually succumbed to the heat and intensity of the inner workings of its once nourishing energy.

This was the new normal.

The planets marched toward their own demise, inevitable was becoming one with the Sun.

With each passing day, things began to change, and mother Earth grew increasingly barren as she became no longer capable of supporting the life which had sprung up under her care.

Everything wilted and died, except for Gaia and her oceans, which did not wilt, but rather, evaporated violently as the ozone became non-existent.

It was a beautiful death.

As such, the last sunset on Earth was one of a kind.

The sky was mixtures of white and gold.

Blistering hot was Mother Earth as she melded with the sun.

It was spectacular as she melted away into both

nothing and everything at the same time.

And yet, it lasted forever, as the Earth was granted a year, a year in which forever was but a moment, and an instant was an eternity.

The Moon beat the Earth by just a few minutes, loving its dance with its partner even up until their final moments.

The Cocktail Party

Mrs. Jacobson always threw the best dinner parties in the neighborhood. She was known to put out her finest china, invite all of the neighbors, and good times were had by all… with the exception of one man at this one particular party, John, who was rather down in the dumps for some reason. Mrs. Jacobson was eyeing the man suspiciously, while he was already in conversation with another neighbor named Robert, and even though Mrs. Jacobson was also in conversation with someone, she was clearly eavesdropping in on their conversation.

"Do you know where she may have gone?" Asked Robert.

"No, Robert, I do not, and I am not quite sure how it is any of your business." Said John, clearly downtrodden.

"Well, it has become quite obvious recently. She hasn't been seen in days and, well… people are beginning to talk."

"Let them talk Robert. They can talk so that I do not have to."

"Well, when people begin to talk, they will ask questions…. and they are going to ask why your wife is missing."

"Your wife is missing?!" Shrieked

Mrs. Jacobson, nearly yelling, clearly loud enough to break through the casual chatter and background music and to reach pretty much everyone in her nearby proximity. The party screeched to a halt as fake conversation ended immediately, and the question they had all been waiting for was finally posed. No longer did the neighborhood association need to fake as if they weren't listening.

John sighed, obviously irritated.

"That's the last time I tell you anything in confidence." He muttered under his breath to Robert, before turning to the rest of them.

"I'm sure she'll turn up eventually. She's never one to miss a cocktail party."

Do Not Disturb

A pair of bloodshot hazel eyes peered through the blinds of a dingy motel bedroom window, looking down from the second floor toward the parking lot, scanning quickly before darting back out of sight behind the cheap plastic covering once more.

A quick tug on Jason's sleeve reminds him that he's not alone.

"Dad, what are you looking for?" Asked the child, just a day over seven years old. Even in his youth, he was acutely aware of the worry in his father's eyes.

"Nothing buddy, just hop back in bed," Jason said, peering once more out of the blinds before turning his attention to the boy who now begrudgingly was climbing back under the covers.

Once settled, the child threw down his arms in exasperation and whined, "But Dad, it's hard to sleep when the Sun is out, and you keep peeling the blinds apart and letting the light come in…"

Jason laughed, knowing full well this sort of stubbornness could only come from his own son. "Just shut your eyes and the light won't get in. It will be night before we know it, and we will be back on the road." The boy sighed but did as he was told, and within a few minutes, the sound of cheap cable TV mixed with the boy's muffled snores, and Jason moved back toward the blinds once more.

This time Jason noticed a new car in the parking lot, and the exceptionally clean black Mercedes Benz he was looking at was not something you would normally see out here deep on the dusty roads of rural West Texas. It made Jason nervous… and so he went to the dresser drawer, pulled out a 9mm Glock pistol, loaded it, and readied it.

A quick glance toward his sleeping son was torn away as boot-steps sounded heavily near the window now, and Jason did not pull back the blinds this time, but rather, he made his way to the door quietly and peered through the peephole. A set of sunglasses stared back at him, and a furious three-round barrage knocked against the door.

"Jason… we know you're in there. Give us the child and everything will just go away."

"Dad?" Came a muffled sound from the boy, now roused, rubbing the crust out of his eyes as he looked toward his father and the sound of the disturbance.

"Look away son." Said Jason, pushing the tip of the gun directly to the peephole. "Everything will be okay."

Thirsty

Aman sits at a bar as the lights of midday stream in through the cracks in the dive's crumbling foundations. The remnants of a glass of flat beer reside on the bar itself, droplets of condensation having already evaporated from it's now room temperature beverage vessel, a half drunk pint ignored by the man drooling with his head in his forearms.

That man was Sam.

"SAM, quit fucking babysitting or leave. Just because you start drinking early that doesn't make this a B&B."

Sam raised his head and looked at the bartender, one of his eyelids noticeably opening much slower than the other.

"What time is it?"

"Time to wake the fuck up, Sunshine."

Sam rested his head back into the puddle of his own drool.

"Is it nice out there today?"

"Every day is as nice as you make it to be."

"Ah, but I smelled rain earlier…"

"For some reason, I would think a bit of hydration would do you a world of good today."

Sam squinted at the bartender. "Did you just call me THIRSTY?"

"Dehydrated, more like."

Sam nodded and raised his head once more, wiping away the drool from his chin before grasping the glass of his lukewarm beer and drinking it down whole, thoroughly quenching his thirst.

"Ahhhhh… Barkeep, you may just be right."

That Special Moment

Everyone's heads turn toward the door at the far end of the church we all are congregating in to witness the most beautiful woman I've ever seen, walking down the aisle with her father, smiling so hard that tears of joy begin to collect near the corners of her eyes.

I return her smile as she nears my seat at the end of the row, and as she passes me it fades back into the standard of my resting bitch face. With that, I begin to daydream and plot my actions.

What I am waiting for is that special moment that all the movies depict.

You know that moment when the priest says to those gathered, "Does anyone have any reason that these two shall not be married?", and at that point, I get up, and shout "I, in fact, DO have a reason that these two should not be married", and out of nowhere comes the ring bearer with a microphone and everyone's attention is suddenly on me.

I tap the microphone to make sure it's on, and it squeals with feedback, making everyone cringe.

I look around and see the confused looks on everybody's face as I, some random girl to them, ruins their entire afternoon, and I surely would have been lost in that moment had not the priest hurried me on with a wave of his hand.

"Father, I object!"

"This is not a courtroom, young lady, just say your piece."

With a gulping of my nerves I begin:

"These two can not be married because no happy marriage can be created when one person is not truly fulfilled. I know this woman, and she knows me, and she should see me standing here with this microphone in my hand and everyone's eyes on me and she should know exactly what it is I am proclaiming."

I turn to her and say, "Do you not remember, dear Elizabeth, that magical night we spent together, all those years ago, the night which awakened in me feelings which I had never known could exist, and in which I took you to a world that this man standing on the altar with you could never hope to crash land on?"

The bride began to blush, and so I continued: "She knows not true love, for true love cannot be realized in but a single night, but must be sustained over the ages, day in and day out, never questioning and never faltering. I am the one that she truly loves, and she knows that deep down in her heart, I am absolutely sure of it, and the look on her face now just strengthens my resolve. Elizabeth, leave this man here on the altar, and run away with me!"

Elizabeth, tears streaming down her face, stretches out her hand to her fiancée, grasping his in hers, and mouths to him, "I am so sorry", as she begins to make her way to me, their fingers lingering on each other until the distance unravels them both.

She moves to me, looking me deep in the eyes, and I grab her by the waist, feeling her hips through her wedding dress, and she leans into me as I grasp her jaw with my other hand and our lips meet in a miraculous moment where everyone claps for true love.

Meanwhile, back in reality, actual clapping snaps me out of my daydream… and as I sit here near the edge of the aisle and witness the love of my life lock lips with her new husband up there on that altar, I realize now that perhaps the moment I was waiting for comes only in the movies.

Another Petal Falls

I bought you a flower today. Not to keep you, or to tell you to be mine, but so that you may watch it wilt and die, the last petal perishing with my final thoughts of you.

So hold still that breath of trouble and toil, as we burn the midnight oil, and find undue reasons to come back to each other, lights flickering on our faces as our fingers tap our screens texting one another. The flirtatious exchange reminds me of that night where the splattering raindrops against my umbrella sounded like firecrackers popping as we kissed under its enveloping embrace.

Dive into the deep end with the master swimmers they said... you'll be fine... there's nothing to worry about.

Meanwhile, thoughts creep to the back of my mind and I remember a good friend saying to me, almost in fated prophecy:

"Did you know you can eat lava? Once."

And oh how that feels reminiscent of this situation now. An incoming paragraph text, with questions about my past and how it affects my integrity. I respond as such:

"I am not the type of man to dwell on the trials and the tribulations of the past, and you could never know them as they were to me, nor am I the type of man to speak of such negativity, and as such you could never know me, as the character of a good man can only be understood by the intuition of that man's soul mate."

The response goes over her head, and she paints me with the most unflattering colors as the picturesque model of someone avoiding the reality of the situation. A few well-timed insults, and I am growing annoyed at this exchange, and my sarcastic nature begins to show:

"And here I am with no tree in sight yet the heavens have graced with me plentiful shade."

She is not a fan, even though she is clearly long-winded. The barrage continues.

I look to the vase in my room, which still holds that flower, and a petal falls in that moment, masterfully illustrating what I could not bring myself to say. As I lay here on my bed, I search the four corners of my ceiling for enlightenment, scouring my brain for something in response…

I have...

Nothing.

Another petal falls.

Withstanding Time

"Son, do you see that hill over there? Yes, that one there, the one that hides the bend of the river from view. Did you know, four generations ago, your great-grandfather fought side by side with his brothers, and won that hill for us? It's ours, all because of him.

No, I wasn't around back then, I'm not that old! Your great-grandfather was a historian, and he wrote down the stories of his times and the victory of his father in the tomes of our people, even detailing the beautiful moment when his father was buried on the very hill that he once risked his life for in combat. That knowledge of our history is ours, all because of him and his efforts, and as of today, that knowledge is yours."

"Dad?"

"Yes, son?"

"How can a hill be ours? Does it not stand self-sufficient, caring not for who thinks themselves its owner?"

He looked toward his son and smiled.

"You are far wiser than your years, my boy… Yes, things which are naturally beautiful, such as that hill, or the ocean to the west of us, or even this moment in time now that we share together, those are things which can never be contained truly by words on a deed. However, do you see on that hill, that tree which is young, like you, yet has begun to stand tall on its own? Your grandfather planted that tree on that hill, many years ago, and even now we can see his impact on this earth, as he found a way to speak to us both in a manner which would withstand the currents of time."

The boy sat and listened quietly for a moment before standing and stretching his limbs in the cool summer breeze.

"Now Dad, is that not something more worthy of a place in our history books?"

Erasmus Falls

Forgive me if my tone is frantic, but I am being chased by a killer.

My name is Erasmus Jones III of Europa Station and should you find this voice memo please return it to my family because these are surely my last moments alive.

I have crash-landed on Pluto, my co-pilot died in the crash, and we are not alone.

I know Firenze died. I saw his helmet cracking and the pressure of non-atmospheric decompression exploding his entire skull against the cabin of our ship. It is not a sight I will ever forget.

However, Firenze is still following me. Yet I know it is not Firenze because I saw Firenze die. But still, when this Firenze pushed me, I fell readily as he caught me wholly unexpected at first. I was so distraught by seeing him that it made no sense to me at all. He rushed me, and I fought back and when I collided with him, it was not actually him but a blob of jelly, and that is really the only way I know how to explain what it was that I had felt, it was as if a massive jellyfish had crawled all over me and yet I still saw only Firenze.

I pushed it away from me, and I ran for my life, and I got away. Then I saw my family. They came to me in the valley of a meteorite crater that I had taken refuge in. I saw my mother, and my father, and my sister, who was only but a child in her falsified visage for she died at that age many years ago and most certainly not on Pluto but on Earth before the Red Giant's expansion and so I know Julia is not here, just as I know that Firenze is not here either, and so when Julia asked me to take off my helmet to come play kickball with her, I did not, and I pushed my dear sister away from me and I ran up the craters far edge and found myself staring over a ridge into a deep ravine.

It was my father who pushed me this time, and I felt the cold jelly once more as I grabbed at him, but the jelly slipped out of my grasp as I fell backwards and then I crashed hard against the bottom, where I most certainly now lay dying, and here I am talking to myself in the darkness, and even now in this moment, in this battered and bruised manner, wheezing as I am reciting this voice memo… I am still sane… sane enough to know that the love of my life, my wife Victoria, is not walking toward me here at the bottom of a ravine on Pluto, without a helmet on, BECAUSE I SAW FIRENZE'S HEAD EXPLODE AND THAT IS NOT A SIGHT I WILL EVER UNSEE.

I am fading now…. but if these are my last words….

My name is Erasmus Jones.

Please tell my family I love them, and tell Victoria…

Do not trust me if you see me alive.

Peter Tigbow

Peter Tigbow was a lonely old man. Twice divorced, he sought the solace of easy, ready to eat, pre-cooked, frozen microwave dinner meals from the local supermarket. Very few steps, even less ingredients, and it made his shopping trips incredibly easy.

You see, Peter Tigbow was always anxious in social situations, even simple ones such as these, like when the store became crowded or he had to bob and weave between baskets in a packed aisle, engagements of that sort were, well, just something he wished had fewer steps and less ingredients. Yet, for some reason, on this shopping trip, the self-checkout line happened to be crowded, and so instead of waiting in line to check himself out, he noticed an uncrowded register lane, and he deposited his basket of microwave dinners upon the automatic grocery belt of a cashier named Roxanne.

She smiled at Peter, and remembered his name from

their last encounter, a couple of months before, right after Peter's divorce, back when he still wore his wedding ring, as not too many men her age dumped basketfuls of microwave dinners for her to scan, and instantly Peter Tigbow knew then not only that he was known as a lonely old man but also he remembered why he favored the self-checkout line at the supermarket recently. He returned the smile, and then hastily rummaged through his wallet for his debit card so he could focus just on the card machine and his PIN number, not the tan line on his ring finger which was beginning to fade, and most certainly not the beautiful woman who had taken notice of him.

"You know you could make this same dish with just a few ingredients don't cha?" She asked, drawing his attention back to her. "It may even save you some money, hun."

"Yes, I guess I could." Said Peter Tigbow, and the conversation ended, having run its course as the sound of his receipt printing filled the space in the dead air.

That night, Peter Tigbow ate his meal in front of the dull blue glow of his big-screen television, and when he was finished, he scraped the leftovers into his trash and on top of the discarded packaging of the frozen meal itself, and the words of Roxanne crept back into his head, and he ruminated on them for the rest of the night.

The next time Peter Tigbow dared to face his social anxiety to once more fulfill his hunter-gatherer instincts at the local supermarket, he opted for a different approach than normal. He walked through the store, not preoccupied with his anxieties, but on a mission to find fresh produce and a nice cut of meat, and if he was feeling adventurous, maybe even a new flavor of ice cream, even if he did quite enjoy the taste of his usual vanilla bean. No, not tonight. Tonight was a mint chocolate chip night.

As he approached aisle 7, he held his head high, and there was Roxanne, and when he placed his groceries on the automatic grocery belt, the change was apparent even to her and she said, "Hey Peter, looks like you're cooking for someone special tonight, huh?"

To which Peter Tigbow replied,

"Just myself, Roxanne."

Please See Attached

Dear Hiring Manager whose name I couldn't find on the job listing,

I am writing with hopes that you may consider my thoughtfully attached .pdf resume which I took many hours personally formatting entirely myself because I really need a job right now, for the position of [Enter job title that we both know I am under qualified for].

Please know that I am a hard-working individual who really has to pay rent soon so I will certainly be a great addition to your team. I can work any day of the week, at any time really since I don't have much of a social life, but like, if you had something where I could start at about 10 or so each day and have weekends off that would be great.

You'll notice once you actually click into my resume that there are a few major gaps in time between jobs, but don't worry about that. I took some time off to be in a band that got mildly famous on YouTube for a little bit but now with that having died down I am totally focused on furthering my career in this [Industry I know nothing about].

I, of course, studied [useless liberal arts degree] at [massively underfunded university] so I know exactly what makes humans do the things that they do, and I can certainly use that experience to help you further the very basic and vague mission statement that I found on your company's website when I briefly googled you before sending this email. "Be the change, see the change" is such an inspiring tagline to me on a personal level because, once again, I don't have a job right now, so if there's anyone who knows about change, it's me.

Literally. I paid my parking ticket last week by scrounging through my couch and smashing my little sister's piggy bank when she wasn't looking. Surprisingly she had quite a bit of money in there, but the cashier at the courthouse wasn't too thrilled with having to count it all. "Lots of pennies," she said. I think that funny anecdote that I just overshared with you certainly qualifies as cash handling experience, which I saw that you were asking for, so you will see that I added that to the list in the skill section with the other buzzwords that I hope you don't ask me about should you call me in for an interview.

Just past that, at the bottom of the short yet somehow still very drawn out resume you will find absolutely zero references, and in their place I have put a section that says, "References available upon request." Please do not request these. The last thing I need is that asshole Richard from my last job telling you that he fired me because I kept coming into work hungover all the time. I mean, c'mon, we both knew I was just there until my mildly successful YouTube career kicked off, Dick, you followed me on Instasnap.

With that said, thank you for taking this time out of your day to review this badly composed resume for the slightly above minimum wage position you posted about on Craigslist yesterday.

Sincerely yours,
Millennial Youth.

Life in Ruins

I can hear a dog barking.

It's the first thing I can remember hearing since my ears stopped ringing. Having what amounts to the top third of a building fall on top of you can do that to your eardrums.

I'm not dying. Not quickly at least. The rubble had landed advantageously around me, and so I am trapped in a small concrete teepee of sorts. I am a little scraped and banged up, but no bones are broken, and the worst thing that I've had to deal with so far is not having much space to designate for a bathroom, and so now not only am I trapped in a tiny wedge between two large slabs of what used to be my office building, but I am huddled in an even smaller section of the already limited space that is not puddled with urine. It smells disgusting, and I'm getting a bit antsy just thinking about it, but, hey, at least I'm still alive. I can thank my nicotine addiction for that.

I don't know if it was an explosion or an earthquake, but whatever it was, the building went down fast. I was in the stairwell on my way down to smoke a cigarette when it happened, when the building swayed and I tumbled down the steps as the walls came with me, and rubble overwhelmed my world, and I submitted to its crumbling embrace, never hearing a single scream or siren. Who knows if they were drowned out at first by the ringing in my head, or if they ended before I woke up…

There was no telling how long I had been down here, trapped in the shattered remains of the fire stairwell. I tried to count the minutes in an hour at one point, but the rhythmic nature of time loses its meaning in absolute darkness.

If it had been only a handful of hours, I would certainly be fine, but if it had been days then I imagine whatever air I have left trapped in the rubble with me could run out soon, and so up until a few moments ago, I had been strongly considering using the last of it to smoke a final cigarette, even if they are all half-broken from breaking my fall. I imagined it would be worth it, I still had my lucky one after all.

Fuck it. If it kills me it kills me. I light one up.

Now that I'm hearing a dog, I'm not regretting my choice.

In a strange way, smoking may have just saved my life.

Raised with Hope

Time and space fractures apart as a fast-moving portal opens, out of which step two men, dressed entirely in black, into the hallway of a hospital's nursery ward. The first through the portal, the older of the two men, had his eyes trained on his forearm, or rather, the holographic user interface which projected from his forearm, which displayed information about their current whereabouts, their vitals, the date and time, among other things.

"Well, it's the correct year, and we both seem to be healthy enough, save an elevated heart rate is all. Now we just need to find the kid."

The second man, his head peeking around the darkened corners of the ward looking for any would-be eavesdroppers, whispered back in return. "You are going to need to explain this to me again… why exactly are you taking him? Won't someone just supplant his place in history? What if you are giving space for someone even more wicked to take power?"

The first man shook his head as he replied, "You can not think that way Jacob, you must only take into account what we know, and what we know is that at this point in his life he is innocent and untainted by the world, and the world itself is unscorched by his impact, and we have a chance to change everything."

"Yeah, yeah, yeah, and it is that same innocence which makes it immoral to just smother him with a pillow, I remember us having that conversation. That is no reason that you must give up your own future, and our time, in exchange for this one. History was not fond of this age, nor this child, do you think to raise him yourself will truly make a difference?"

The first man stopped walking, having made it to the small nursery where the infants of the hospital slept quietly in the still midnight hour.

"The Laws of Time Travel forbid bringing anything from the past back with us. And so, my options are to either kill the child, return back to our age, and have to live with the memory of having killed this young boy with my bare hands, for a potential future that I will never know, or I stay here, in this time, and I raise young Adolf myself and see if the universe which diverges from our own timeline is one in which hate of the magnitude he unleashed upon the world is never allowed to foster and breed. To me, the answer is clear."

Jacob sighed as his mentor walked away from him toward the crib of the child, knowing full well that the decision had already been made, and so he raised his arm out in front of him and once more ripped a hole in space and time.

With one last look over his shoulder as he entered the portal, his eyes glanced back to the young child as he was lifted from his bed, and Jacob spoke, less to his mentor, and more to the universe...

"Do not lose hope should nothing change."

Self Revelations through Haiku

I unlock my door, throw my keys to the floor, fling off my shoes, and throw myself onto the bed. Then, exasperated and in combat with myself, I rose from my duvet grave and walked my way to my desk, as the typewriter which was revealed when my lamp's light flickered to a start, taunted me as I began to write:

I am frustrated
with the aspects of my life
framed by hands unknown

Nope, not it. Crumpled paper hits the wastebasket and keys pound again.

Accepting a life
with an undervalued self
is to be denied

My forehead slams against the faux maple veneer of my desk in an aggressively rhythmic fashion, as I wrap fresh paper around the platen and slam my digits against the keys in a similarly harmonious accord.

The mind is a tool
made powerful by only
the thoughts it allows

A sigh escapes lips that are unable to craft the words which are lost to the universe. I begin again.

Take my soul toward
space where it is capable
of well-deserved love.

And then,

Fuck haikus and I
Two things crafted by me
and undone in kind.

I am running out of paper. I am also running out of time before she gets home.

Dear, I ran away
Not because you were not loved
but to find myself

Too cliché.

I am ashamed of
nothing but the search for what
you see in my eyes

Then, as if I had been struck by lightning, a realization came to mind, to which I write:

You do not have to
deserve something to make it
present in your life

And so, I picked myself up from my desk, and as my beautiful wife walked through the threshold of our home, I kissed her with true love, and then I took out the trash, filled with scraps of thoughts undeserving of the life we have built together.

Home

Undone by the wayward wind, her rainbow-colored ribbon floated helplessly adrift the breeze which burst forth across the bow of the ferry, which itself had set across the bay toward San Francisco. Lacking the now airborne fabric, unkempt was her hair, though that seemed to be her mainstay, save for the few tufts tucked behind her ears. Her eyes scanned the skyline, for on the horizon lay the big city, shrouded in fog, and yet it made clear the answer to her dreams of a new life all on her own. No more overly controlling mother, no more unaccepting father, no more of the same old Mr. Not Quite Right, and certainly no more dreading her small-town existence anymore.

Today was a new day, and with a new city would certainly come its up and downs, just as the bobbing of the ferry reminded her, and yet, she was ready for the trials and tribulations of her new adventure. As they slowed and pulled into shore, she quickly gathered her over the shoulder bag as well as her bursting at the seams suitcase, the pink one with the one funky wheel that never seemed to mind its manners, and she disembarked, for once not minding a slow single filed line as she walked down the ramp and over the dock plate.

The bustle of the Embarcadero was a sight to see for the small-town girl, having come from the dull existence and day to day monotony of a middle-class suburb not even worth the time or energy of speaking its name. San Francisco, home of the freaks and weirdos, which she gladly sought to embrace.

The cab ride from the waterfront to her new home in The Castro was not one that she would ever forget, as she found her first glimpse of the city which gave her hope of acceptance and opportunity, more than she had ever imagined. The skyscrapers gleamed in the rays of sunlight which pierced the foggy canopy coming off the bay, the people hustled and busted on their way, and as she continued down Market Street, people… were living on the street.

She put her hand against the glass window of the yellow cab, streaking it with her fingertips, and her breath cast its own foggy veil across her sight line. She wiped it away, though the vision was not as easily erased. Men in suits, talking on the most sophisticated of cell phones, could not be bothered by the white noise of class inequality as they sidestepped their inconvenient truths.

As the scene of the metropolis' downtown faded from view, she sank back into her seat and sighed, realizing now that her own future was not guaranteed. Having moved here with but a summer's worth of savings and the two bags that sat next to her in this cab, she had nothing but her own wits and grit to sustain her now. Everything she had dreamed of, the big city fantasy was here before her, but so was the harsh visage of reality, and she knew it would not be easy.

Nevertheless, as the cab pulled up to her brightly colored apartment building, atop which flew the flag of her people… she smiled.

She was finally home.

The Union of Fire & Ice

She was a fire woman and he a man made from ice. They knew with no hesitation that their meeting had changed their lives.

He tried to play it cool as she placed him under her warm embrace, but then, he cracked, his frozen shell vulnerable as the heat of their passion began to have him start melting for her. In a sudden response, she pushed him away and looked at her flames in a shamble of shame, afraid of how her combustible nature had so abruptly consumed him.

To his character, he reached out to grasp her hand anyway, and when she accepted him he pulled her closer, and his state of being transformed, for with her he was different, not better nor worse, but different, and this he knew would happen and yet he did not care, as he doubted he could ever go back to the ice-cold existence he once lived without her.

Water began to drip from the cracks she had made in his hardened exterior, and those droplets sizzled against her, changing her as well, and in some ways, putting her own brilliant blaze in jeopardy, though that was, of course, never his intention, yet still between them a hazy steam had risen in the air. The fog of love had painted everything obscured. She looked up and wondered if floating toward the heavens was a mixture of them both.

She was worried, not only that she was consuming him, but that she was losing herself when the water enveloped her, and yet, she felt him as a sudden chill rushed up her spine. His touch was a new experience for her, one unlike any other she had known before.

As the image of him emerged from the steam, his face glistening like glaciers in the summer Sun, with fresh droplets of condensation already streaming down his frosted brow, it was in that moment she saw him for the man he truly was, having risked his solid existence to hold her so close to him. She pushed herself against him in kind, knowing she would gladly risk the same to find a new life together.

His voice instilled her with his stone-cold resolve as he whispered in her ear:

"My beautiful burning flame, let us be together as one, as you see my ice turns to water when you burn bright as the Sun. In this new state of being, you are not fading but changing, raising us both so much higher than we could ever have soared. Our home in the sky will be a noble golden cumulus, and I ask: Oh my dear, won't you evaporate with me? Do not be afraid, to me you will always be that brightly burning flame, and know that even though I am melting I shall not be absorbed, nor shall we be as before, but trust me that the future shall see us work together to make us a droplet of rain. So what say you, my love, should we stay frozen and flames?"

She felt the same, for true wildfires can not be sustained, so they fell into each other, and they rose to live up in the clouds, one day changing into the rain, which they hoped with a bit of good timing, and having sewed the right seeds, that the union of fire and ice could sprout forth something unlike them both, and perhaps even more.

Hark! A Thief in the Night!

Chorus: "Hark! A thief in the night!"

Homeowner: "Upon what means does this dastardly trespasser invite himself to traverse across the sacred space of my hearth! Dare not to step one toe further within, or I swear to the gods above that I shall smite you down where you stand!"

Trespasser: "Oh, woe is me, the lowly thief, alas, I have been seen! For those same gods have destined me to meet today with failure, but oh what have I done to be selected as the lesser?! Dearest Fates, please spare me from the consequences of my actions, for I am but a product of my circumstances, a good man gone wrong in the pursuit of a better life, and you should know that I plead for forgiveness... and perhaps a path into the night!"

H: "You ask of forgiveness, and I ask that you waste not the time of the heavens with your insincere pleas since we both know you would not have forgiven my home of your larcenous ways had I been the one pleading for you to flee into the night…"

T: "Then what do you suggest, oh noble lord, shall I slide myself onto the end of your butcher knife? Or do I back away, back to my meager existence, and you back to the wealth of yours? Or rather yet, shall we have a cup of tea as we await the proper authorities?"

H: "Do not mock me, scoundrel! I could end you now and have the law on my side, for have thou not read the castle doctrine?"

T: "Have thou not read that the people can not read?!"

H: "Ah, I have read that indeed… so go now thief, go on there to the bookshelf, and steal yourself a book before you steal into the night, and perhaps then you can learn to obey the laws we write therein!"

T: "But sir, a book to me holds such little value, for I have just told you that I can not read, nor can my hungry offspring be sustained by paper or words, so what say of you to some bread instead?"

H: "Begone you beggar!"

Under the Light of the Red Giant

The walls crumbled after a century of conflict.

The cries of statesmen and widows and orphans accompanied the trumpets declaring the people's freedom.

Footsteps of soldiers made the earth quake under their might.

The chants of the enlightened rose up against them.

The intellectuals receded to their secret circles, knowing well what would come next, a new system, a new culture, a new King to worship or be labeled a heretic and sentenced to die. If you were lucky, you may just end up in jail, imprisoned to hard labor for the rest of your days.

Not everyone knows how the Earth may end. It is what you make of your time here that truly matters.

Life does not guarantee you luck.

Life does not guarantee you anything.

The astrologists looked toward the stars for guidance. The scientists looked as far as they could, in hopes to secure the future of their people.

*

*

*

*   *

A young boy stood on Earth, hurtling around the Sun, growing older with every rotation.

He looked up toward the stars, imagining himself as one of those celestial beings…

Loving them eternally…

Their warmth felt from a galaxy away.

In this Universe, the people made the best with what they had. Their own principles decided the fate of mankind, one in which the history of their species could be weighed without penance needed. Some thought they had achieved a world in which their children could grow up and have a fighting chance. Others did not, wary of the destination, enthralled by false prophets that declared the end of the world.

In spite of everything, the happy couple kissed on the beach as the Sun set, not a care in the world, having just announced to their friends and family that they were having a baby girl.

A Note from the Author

I would just like to offer my humblest thanks and appreciation for the moments you have spent reading my words. The Sunday Stories got me through the darkest depths of the Coronavirus lockdown in 2020, and to be able to share the messages of hope which kept me going then with you now, is a gift beyond my wildest dreams.

This piece of work initially started as a workshop for me. Something that I could pour time into in an attempt to break free of the dread and monotony of the lockdown. It all took place over the course of 18 weeks from March 22 to July 19, and it encapsulated a time in my life in which everything that San Francisco was experiencing became overwhelming to deal with. All I could do was to remain positive and keep myself hopeful.

In an effort to build toward something outside of the work on my core trilogy of novels, I decided to undertake the writing task of creating stories entirely within one day each week. Weekly obligations pushed aside,

I dedicated Sundays to this task and swore to maintain that schedule in a challenge to myself, not truly knowing what might come from it. The only premise was that the stories must be completed solely within the day.

They were stories of love and lost love, and fear and hopelessness, and hope and looking toward the future, and not letting the past dictate that future, and everything in between. They were simply feelings escaping me in a way that I could not express to the outside world or anyone in my life at the time. I was screaming at The Universe through text on pages. I was alone and afraid and yet still forced to be strong and keep productive. In reality, this collection of stories mixed with the manual rhythm of a Royal Quiet Deluxe typewriter was a simple case of me processing my own humanity in the face of a global pandemic. These stories kept me going each week. I am certain we all know the effects that year had on us, and I hope moving forward we can remain positive in light of all the hardships we have faced.

If you felt my soul through these pages just know I will be writing until the day I die.

If you would like to keep up with me in the future, I would like to direct you to SFwordsmith.com where you can find updates on projects I am working on, exclusive short stories, blogs about my life in San Francisco, upcoming novels, and series.

Once again thank you for your time and I hope you

have enjoyed the Sunday Stories.

   –Spencer Spalding

Lore Appendix

SPOILER ALERT: (Please do not read this section before finishing your first full read-through of The Sunday Stories)

Since this collection of individual flash fiction scenes happened over the course of 18 weeks, at first the stories were separate pieces that had no true connection to each other. However, as the series went on, it became clear to me that I was subconsciously intermingling some of the stories into a shared universe. In case you did not pick up on it from your first read-through, I would like to point out a few things which were not explicitly stated, but that I have come to accept as parts of the underlying lore of the Sunday Stories Universe.

• Tanner and Sara from Echoes of the Night are the same couple watching the sunset at the end of the book in Under the Light of the Red Giant. They are also the couple featured on the cover art. Sara once more makes an appearance by herself in Life in Ruins. A habitual smoker, when Sara became pregnant, she quit, choosing to be hopeful for the future even in light of Earth's potential outcome. Tanner makes appearances in Another Petal Falls and Self Revelations through Haiku, at points undone by their miscommunications, but choosing to love his wife nonetheless.

• In That Special Moment, when the couple got married, no one spoke to dissent on their union. Home, which comes later on in the series, details the early life of the girl who did not speak up at their wedding. She is also the missing wife from the cocktail party having left her life to run away to San Francisco.

• The Red Giant's expansion was at first just meant to be a story of the death of Earth. I found it to be a beautiful expression of the uncertainty of life and it felt impactful to describe what might happen in that situation in a way that did not involve humanity. Yet with that being the second story that I wrote in the series, moving forward I always had a creeping thought of… what if these stories are all taking place in a Universe in which… well, no one knows quite yet that the Sun is about to expand, taking them all with it? That impending unknown helped to keep each story encapsulated in their own specific moments of time, which allowed the stories to draw out the beauty of those singular moments. In a vastly different regard, the last story, Under the Light of the

Red Giant, clearly indicates the implications of humanity realizing what is happening to their home and the varied reactions one might have to such news.

• After it is first mentioned, the impact of the Red Giant's expansion is not noted again until you find Erasmus Jones on Pluto, with humanity having escaped to the moons of Jupiter in an attempt to save themselves from the expansion. Sent on a recon mission looking for new resources, humanity has made their way to the dwarf planet and crash-landed there. Who, or what, attacked Erasmus and his co-pilot, Firenze, we do not know.

• The idea that the events of Raised with Hope, (stealing the young child and attempting to change history) could have some way altered the course of history and changed the timeline into one in which allowed us to survive the Red Giant expansion is something that also was at the back of my mind, but was not something that I felt was necessary to expand upon in this book. Some things are left best to the imagination... or perhaps, volume 2. With that said, the young boy and his father in Do Not Disturb are indeed the stolen child and the Mentor from Raised with Hope. On the run for crimes against Humanity, and chased by Time Police, Jason does his best to protect his new son and raise him to be a man of integrity.

• Near the end of the series, The Union of Fire & Ice was actually meant to be a story of the beginning of life on Earth in this Universe, with The Red Giant, at the beginning of the book, illustrating its death. Every other story, with the sole exception of Erasmus Falls, is placed chronologically between these two events.

If you would like to read the book in Chronological Order, it would be somewhat as follows:

The Union of Fire & Ice
Withstanding Time
Hark! A Thief in the Night!
Raised with Hope
Do Not Disturb
Thirsty
Peter Tigbow
The Cocktail Party
Home
Please See Attached
Echoes of the Night
Another Petal Falls
Life in Ruins
That Special Moment
Self Revelations Through Haiku
The Red Giant / Under the Light of the Red Giant
Erasmus Falls

As for the order of the stories, I decided to present the series as they were originally released, with very few alterations to how I wrote them each Sunday during the lockdown. It was a hell of a run coming up with and writing these stories each week, so I like to have first-time readers figure it out just as I did. They are all separate stories which can be held to their own storylines, or when taken as a whole they are part of a much wider Universe which is ebbing and flowing in reaction to itself. If you go back now and reread it, especially in the original order, you will have these added character insights that show you a whole new Universe that was right before your eyes the entire time.

I hope you can get as lost in the Universe as I did. Perhaps we will return one day.

About the Author

SPENCER SPALDING is a novelist and poet from San Francisco, California. Raised in various parts of the Northern Bay Area of California, as well as the rural landscapes of East Texas, Spencer receives his inspiration from the beauty of the Universe at large.

He finds himself drawn toward creating short stories, flash fiction, novels, songs, and poetry all of which seek to incorporate ideals of love, elements of nature, and glimpses into the experience of humanity.

Spencer received his Bachelor of Arts degree in Ancient History from San Francisco State University. His studies focused on Ancient Mediterranean Cultures, their architecture, their art, and their works of literature, which eventually lead him to pursue a minor in Classical Studies. He used the skills he learned from his professors to read the classics in their ancient scripts in an effort to better understand epic literature and its impact on the world. Spencer sees himself as a student of the great historians, philosophers, poets, and orators of the Ancient World.

"Without the words of Plato, Aristotle, Virgil, Homer, Socrates and other great minds from the Classical world, I would not be the man I am today, nor would I ever be the type of writer that I strive to become."

For now, Spencer Spalding can be found on the western side of San Francisco, watching the Sun set over the Pacific Ocean, dreaming of the words for his next novel.

https://sfwordsmith.com